Tim the Trumpet

Blackie Bears

Tim the Trumpet

Elisabeth Beresford

Illustrated by Victoria Cooper

A Blackie Bear

*To all the children at Ormer House,
Alderney*

BLACKIE CHILDREN'S BOOKS

Published by the Penguin Group
Penguin Books Ltd, 27 Wrights Lane, London W8 5TZ, England
Penguin Books USA Inc., 375 Hudson Street, New York, New York 10014,
USA
Penguin Books Australia Ltd, Ringwood, Victoria, Australia
Penguin Books Canada Ltd, 10 Alcorn Avenue, Toronto, Ontario, Canada
M4V 3B2
Penguin Books (NZ) Ltd, 182–190 Wairau Road, Auckland 10, New Zealand

Penguin Books Ltd, Registered Offices: Harmondsworth, Middlesex,
England

First published 1992

1 3 5 7 9 10 8 6 4 2

Text copyright © 1992 Elisabeth Beresford
Illustrations copyright © 1992 Victoria Cooper

The moral right of the author has been asserted

Made and printed in Great Britain by BPCC Hazells Ltd, Member of
BPCC Ltd

A CIP catalogue record for this book is available from the British Library

ISBN 0 216 93298 X

About the Author

Elisabeth Beresford is an established children's author. Although this is her first book for Blackie in the Blackie Bear series, she has written over one hundred books, including the enormously popular Wombles series. She is a freelance writer and journalist, and has frequently broadcast on television and radio. She has also spent time in Africa, giving talks to children in schools. Although she was born in Paris, Elisabeth now lives on Alderney, in the Channel Islands. In between her writing she even finds time to work as a Station Master on the Alderney Railway!

To look at, Tim was a perfectly
ordinary boy. His hair stood up
on end and his face was never
quite clean. His jeans were
definitely dusty and his T-shirt
always managed to be back to
front. But all this could happen to
anyone. What made Tim quite,
quite different from anybody else
was his voice.

7

Tim's voice was truly amazing. It was like a cross between a factory hooter and a foghorn. Or perhaps a roll of thunder and a ship's siren. And there was nothing he could do about it. It was just something he had been born with. His parents, of course, noticed his voice right from the start.

When Tim was a baby he
would, like any other baby, let
out a cry to tell everybody that he
wasn't happy. Only it wasn't so
much a cry, it was more like—
well—an alarm bell going off. It
certainly alarmed the neighbours.
They used to gather in the street
outside the house, and discuss in

worried whispers whether they ought to call the police. They were certain something terrible was happening!

Tim's parents had to explain over and over again. 'No really, it's nothing. It's just that Tim doesn't want to have his bath . . .' or 'Tim just wants more breakfast . . .' And then, 'It's his voice you see. Tim has this very, very loud voice . . .'

The neighbours got used to it after a while. They just shut their windows against the occasional roar. Even so, when Tim was christened, the Vicar—who had been warned beforehand—wisely wore ear muffs.

Soon Tim was old enough to have his loud voice explained to him. He knew that his voice was, well, just slightly different from the other children. He really did try very hard not to roar or bellow. But it was no good. He just could *not* control his amazing voice.

When he went to Play School for the first time the other children were scared of him.

When he fell over and banged his knee he couldn't help crying. But all the other children ran for the far corners of the room with their hands over their ears. Then, of course, *they* all began to cry, although not as loudly as Tim. It was very, very difficult. Tim had to learn to be braver than anybody else so that he didn't cry, no matter what happened.

But that still left his speaking voice. There was only one thing for it. He had to whisper, and even that had a kind of ring to it. By the time he went to proper school Tim had a nickname. He was known throughout the neighbourhood as Tim the Trumpet!

When Tim moved on to his next school he was put at the very furthest corner of the room. His teacher asked him to reply to questions in a whisper. It was very difficult because when he *did* know an answer Tim wanted to shout it out. Instead he had to sit with his hand over his mouth.

14

The other children still kept well away from him, so poor Tim felt a bit down in the dumps.

One morning, Tim's Sports Master, Mr Daniels, came up to him.

'Tim?' he said. Tim nodded. He was kicking a ball round the playground in break. He would have liked to play with the others, but as usual they had all gone off and left him.

'I thought,' said Mr Daniels, 'that you might be just the one I am looking for.'

Tim brightened up.

'I think you are just the person I need to help me referee the football.'

16

It was better than nothing so Tim nodded again.

'See you at three this afternoon down at the pitch,' said Mr Daniels and he went off whistling.

Tim was down at the pitch by five to three. Mr Daniels explained what he wanted Tim to do. As the players came onto the

pitch they looked sideways at
Tim as if to say, 'You're not one
of us. What are *you* doing here?'

They soon found out. A player
happened to stray over the line.
Tim took a deep breath.

'OFF SIDE!' he shouted
happily. He hadn't been able to
shout so loud for ages!

The players stopped dead and stood like statues. Every single bird in the neighbourhood went flapping and squawking into the sky. One of the teachers who had been cycling past fell off her bicycle. Even Mr Daniels, who had been prepared for Tim's voice, nearly swallowed his whistle. He ran over to Tim, a little pale, while the statues slowly came back to life.

'Not *quite* so loud, please Tim,' said Mr Daniels.

It was a shame really because Tim hadn't enjoyed a good shout for a long time. Still, half a shout was better than no shout at all. So Tim nodded.

Once he got the hang of it he did very well. There was a THROW IN, at least three PENALTYS and a splendid FOUL. The guilty player turned as red as a brick!

But, of course, it didn't make Tim any more popular with the others. They still either kept well away from him or they teased him, so Tim still felt very lonely. Tim felt even more unhappy when he found out that at half term his form were going off camping. They were going for a long weekend beside the sea, which sounded great!

Then Tim thought, 'I shan't be asked' and he went mooching off

round the playground. His mouth
was turned right down at the
corners like a shovel. Mr Daniels,
who was in charge of the
camping, glanced out of the
window and saw Tim. He
guessed right away what the
trouble was. He decided that
minute to invite Tim to go on the
camping weekend. He opened the
window and called out.

23

'Tim, can you come here a moment? I want to talk to you about the camping weekend.'

Tim couldn't wait to tell his parents that at the very last minute he'd been asked to join the camping weekend. His parents were nearly as excited as he was. They looked up on the map exactly where he was going. His father told him a dozen times that he simply must keep a scarf over

his mouth as much as possible, just in case he forgot about his voice.

Tim grinned from ear to ear and nodded.

On the morning of the camping weekend, all the children were shouting and laughing. It was impossible for poor Mr Daniels to get twelve children into the minibus, let alone leave on time!

He didn't quite tear his hair out, but he got very near it. He shouted 'Quiet' until his voice went hoarse. Nobody could hear him as everybody (except Tim) was talking at once! In despair he looked at Tim. Tim understood and took a deepish breath.

'QUI . . . ET!' he shouted.

The minibus driver nearly jumped out of his skin. There was complete silence. It was uncanny. Mr Daniels just pointed at the bus and everybody got on without speaking a word. Of course it didn't last but at least they only left thirty-five minutes late. The driver kept his shoulders hunched right up to his ears as though he

was trying to be invisible. Tim
didn't notice, he was too busy
with his nose pressed to the
window. He had even
remembered to put his scarf over
his mouth.

The camp site was quite small with only ten tents, a small shop and a shower block. It was in a sort of sandy field with only a big grass bank between it and the sea. There was a large flat beach with rocks which curved round at each end so that it was very nearly a lake. But what really caught everybody's attention was that the right hand rocks led out to a tiny island. It just begged to be explored!

'No!' said Mr Daniels, to a chorus of Can we explore? Can we explore? from all the children. 'Unpack, put your sleeping bags out, then supper and AFTER THAT BED!'

He still sounded a bit hoarse.

Tim woke up before any of the others in the morning. He was in the last tent so it was quite easy for him to climb out of his sleeping bag, pull on some clothes and to wander off to explore without anyone else knowing. It would have been more fun to explore with other people, but that couldn't be helped. He didn't even bother to take the scarf with him. He climbed the bank and then, kicking sand in all directions, walked along the shore to have a look at the tiny island. The sea was streaming out, leaving all kinds of interesting things behind it. There were

plastic buckets, an old boot, a
very dead crab, squelchy brown
seaweed and a lot of cuttle fish.
There was a decidedly fishy
smell, and some large grey and
white gulls came stalking over to
have a look. At the end of the
straggling line was a gull which
seemed to have been left behind,
but was pretending not to care.

31

Tim half hoped he might find
some amazing treasure so he
could dazzle the others, but all he
found was a very old trainer. It
was odd how people seemed to
lose just one shoe. What
happened to the other one?

After breakfast (delicious) there
was tidying-up (boring) followed
by swimming (extremely cold to
begin with, but it got better).

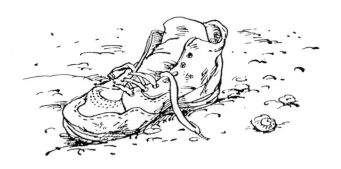

Everybody was having a great
time except Tim who still felt on
the edge of everything. He felt
like the one gull who always
seemed to get left behind by all
the others.

   After lunch seemed a perfect
time to explore the small island.

   'Aren't you coming too, Tim?'
asked Mr Daniels.

   But Tim only shook his head.

He would have loved to go exploring, but even more than that he needed a good shout or he'd go quite dotty!

'Suit yourself,' said Mr Daniels, 'but don't go too far away and no swimming on your own.'

Tim watched until the explorers had crossed the narrow and deep gulley which separated the beach from the island. Then he was off in the opposite direction along the sand, his feet flying, and up the far rocks. The gulls marched out of his way and the one which got left behind all the time had to hop to catch up.

Tim reached a good craggy rock, settled his feet firmly on a

ledge and looked round the
deserted beach. Then he opened
his mouth, took a deep breath
and . . . SHOUTED!

It was quite amazing the effect
Tim's voice had on the birds.
They went straight up in the air,
wheeled round and round in a
great circle and then headed out
over the waves. Further out to

sea, shags and cormorants
flapped heavily away. Two terns
which had been diving for fish
decided to look elsewhere. Tim
felt quite good, as though he was
the Master of the Beach. He had
another two shouts and then went
off to do some exploring of his
own, climbing up a steep path
which led to a grass ledge. Just
the place for one final last shout
before going back to camp . . .

The gulls were just starting to
fly back in a rather cautious way.
Tim let them come all the way
back before he let rip again. The
gulls turned away, just as they
had before and headed out
towards the little island. Then a
very strange thing happened.

Suddenly they turned round and started to fly back towards him, very low over the water. And then, stranger still, Tim saw that the small island had vanished. It just wasn't there any more. In fact there was nothing there at all. Just whiteness. All Tim could see now was the white rolling mist.

The sea was coming in fast and the whiteness was coming with it. The gulls landed on the beach, ruffling up their feathers and hunching themselves backwards and forwards. They even let the small, straggling gull join them. They seemed very nervous and Tim began to feel the same.

There was something strange and mysterious about this great white, swirling, silent sea mist. Rocks and waves vanished in seconds.

Tim decided to make for the camp at once. He was already halfway along the beach when he thought of the others. It wouldn't be much fun being stuck out on an invisible island with the sea coming in. They wouldn't be able to see their way back, and they would be stranded because the gulley would fill up. They might even miss tea and it was getting distinctly chilly with the sun blotted out.

Tim looked round for

somebody, anybody, to help him.
But there *wasn't* anybody. Even
the gulls were starting to follow
him about as if they were glad of
his company. What was he to do?
How could he get them back?
They'd be lost in that thick,
swirling mist. Tim paused. A
little wave came lapping in at his
feet, making the seaweed slurp
about.

'Wow,' said Tim and the sound of his own voice made him jump.

It was then he got his great idea. Tim made for the bit of the beach which he reckoned was closest to the invisible island. He took the deepest breath of his life and . . .

SHOUTED
and
SHOUTED
and
SHOUTED!

His amazing voice hit the mist, got a bit muffled, but travelled on and on and on until it reached Mr Daniels and the rest of the explorers. They were all huddled together in a chilly, anxious

waists. Then they were on rocks
again. But by this time the shouts
were very hoarse indeed. So
hoarse, in fact, they were almost
a wheeze. And then, at last, there
was sand under their feet and no
sea. They were back in the real,
proper world!

Tim was down on his hands and
knees, exhausted, surrounded by
gulls who were watching him
anxiously. Everybody talked at
once and hit Tim on the back and
said he was the best human
lighthouse in the world, and he
could have two helpings of tea,

and they would have had to
spend hours on the island if it
hadn't been for him.

'I think I speak for all of us,'
said Mr Daniels, interrupting the
hubbub of voices, 'when I say
that in future you can shout as
much as you like. OK?

Tim opened his mouth, and shut it again. Nothing happened!

'Tim?' said everybody, 'Tim? Shout at us. Tim!'

But for the first time in his life Tim couldn't. All that he could manage was a croaky whisper. Everybody, even the gulls, crowded round to encourage him.

But it was no good. Tim the Trumpet was silent.

At least for the time being . . .